Previously in the Agent Alfie series:

Thunder Raker

ichards, Justin.
orted! /

009.
33052282 25
i   09/09/13

AGENT ALFIE

SORTED!

Justin Richards

Illustrations by Jim Hansen

HarperCollins *Children's Books*

First published in Great Britain by HarperCollins *Children's Books* 2009

HarperCollins *Children's Books* is a division of
HarperCollins*Publishers* Ltd
77-85 Fulham Palace Road, Hammersmith, London W6 8JB

The HarperCollins *Children's Books* website address is
www.harpercollins.co.uk

3

Text copyright © Justin Richards 2009

Justin Richards asserts the moral right to be identified
as the author of this work

ISBN 978-0-00-727358-4

Printed and bound in England by
Clays Ltd, St Ives plc

Conditions of Sale
This book is sold subject to the condition that it shall not, by way of
trade or otherwise, be lent, re-sold, hired out or otherwise circulated
without the publisher's prior written consent in any form of binding
or cover other than that in which it is published and without a
similar condition including this condition being imposed on the
subsequent purchaser.

Mixed Sources
Product group from well-managed
forests and other controlled sources
www.fsc.org   Cert no. SW-COC-1806
© 1996 Forest Stewardship Council

FSC is a non-profit international organisation established to promote the
responsible management of the world's forests. Products carrying the FSC
label are independently certified to assure consumers that they come
from forests that are managed to meet the social, economic and
ecological needs of present and future generations.

Find out more about HarperCollins and the environment at
www.harpercollins.co.uk/green

For Julian – Senior Agent.

Welcome to Thunder Raker Manor

An Introduction to the School
by Mr Trenchard, Head Teacher

Thunder Raker Manor is an exclusive school for boys and girls from 8 to 18. Some of the children come daily, some are boarders. Some of them I remember, some of them I— er, what was I saying?

Anyway, all our students are here because their parents or guardians are connected with the Security Services. Spies and agents are happy to send their children to Thunder Raker Manor secure in the knowledge that they will be safe from any possible threats.

We teach a full curriculum at Thunder Raker, fully compliant with the National Thingummy. And alongside the English and Maths and History and Geography, our students learn skills that may just come in handy back home or in their future careers

— if they have inherited their parents' inclinations and aptitudes.

As well as being an honorary CT (Classified Training) Academy, Thunder Raker is especially pleased with its latest SATS results. We take the Special Agent Training Standards very seriously indeed and have achieved excellent levels in Surveillance, Code Breaking and Sabotage.

And if the Security Services need a bit of help from some youngsters for a special mission, or if the villainous agents of that dastardly organisation known only as the Secret Partners for Undertaking Destruction (SPUD) try to take over the school or kidnap one of the teachers — rest assured, every one of our students is ready and prepared.

Mr Trenchard has been the Head Teacher of Thunder Raker Manor since Mrs Muldoom's unfortunate accident on the assault course all those years ago. He is superbly qualified and takes great pride in his work. When he can remember what it is. Very good — carry on. Um. Yes...

Mr Trenchard

Colonel Hugh Dare-Swynne's Class of the Week

This week the Colonel focuses on Class 3D, which is taught by Miss Jones.

Miss Jones

Miss Jones says:

3D is a lovely class and works hard. This year was especially exciting for everyone as we had a new student start — Alfie (surname classified). Alfie is already settling in very well, and even has his own cover story — some nonsense about his father actually being a postman. As if!

Alfie fits in well with the other children. He is nine years old, and he's a clever, practical boy with lots of common sense. He's brave and loyal and fun. Though I have to say he doesn't always quite understand some of the lessons or the way we do things here at Thunder Raker. But his common sense approach is a breath of fresh air and he sees the world — and our problems — in a much less cluttered and complicated way than the other children.

Jack

Next up is Jack. Jack's dad is head of the Secret Service, though of course we don't mention that. But it does explain why Jack's a bit full of himself. He is always coming up with terrific ideas and plans, though usually they are rather impractical and just too involved ever to work.

Harry

Harry's dad has infiltrated SPUD and
sends him strange, coded text messages
and letters written in invisible ink.
Sometimes the children have to go and
rescue or help him, which cuts into the
school day. Harry isn't the brightest of
the bunch by a long way, but his
questions often throw up problems with
Jack's ideas. He is brave and loyal and
willing and likes doing PE — on the
school assault course.

Sam
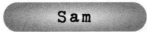

Sam's mum works in Whitehall for
Hush Hush, designing equipment for
agents and spies. Sam uses a
motorised wheelchair — which looks
ordinary but has amazing gadgets
built into it. Sam's mum made him
his wheelchair because the NHS
one didn't have a very good
anti-missile protection system.
And one of the wheels was wonky.

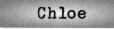

Moving on to the girls, Chloe is the daughter of a renowned spy (and doesn't she know it). If you thought Jack was a bit full of himself, he's got nothing on Chloe. She just has to be the centre of attention, wearing the latest fashion — and spying — accessories. At home she's got her telly wired up with a Playstation 3, a Wii, and the very latest omni-processing decryptortron. Unfortunately Alfie isn't terribly impressed by all this, so he and Chloe haven't really hit it off.

Alice

Alice's dad is a double agent (but it's a bit unclear which side he's actually on). You never know where you are with Alice — she says one thing then does another. Her moods are volatile and she's got a temper like a tank-buster missile when it goes off.

Beth

Beth is a swot and a techie. Her dad is a
super-boffin who runs the Government's
Inventing Taskforce (GIT). She's inherited
his absented-minded braininess. She's not
so hot on the practical side of things
though — she can design a robot to tie your
shoelaces, but she's always tripping over
her own feet. She comes to school on her
rocket-powered rollerblades.

A Passion for Excellence

Miss Jones

Miss Jones is responsible for teaching
Class 3D the ordinary everyday subjects
like Maths and English and History. She's
newly qualified, quiet and unassuming.
Like Miss Jones, all the subject teachers
at Thunder Raker Manor are fully
qualified and at the very peak of their
profession. Many of them are former
agents and spies, so together they bring
a wealth of experience to the school.

Mr Cryption

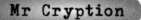

Mr Cryption teaches Codes.
He's tall and thin and no one
understands anything he says.

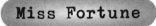

Miss Fortune

Miss Fortune teaches Assassination. Her classes always seem to be a few pupils short — they get sent on errands or asked to help fetch something, and never come back... Note, though, that Class 3D is too young for Assassination, which is only taught in the Sixth Form.

Sir Westerly Compass

Sir Westerly Compass is in charge of Tracking Skills. He's always late for class, and his lessons are often moved at short notice.

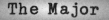

The Major — that's all he's ever called — is in charge of Sabotage Training. He has an enormous moustache and he's rather accident prone. Everything he touches breaks — even the plate he gets his school dinner on...

Mrs Nuffink

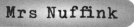

Mrs Nuffink teaches Surveillance. Don't mess around in her class — she's got eyes in the back of her head. No, really.

Mr Trick

Camouflage is supposed to be taught by Mr Trick. But no one can find him.

Reverend "Bongo" Smithers

The Chaplain is Reverend "Bongo" Smithers, a former fighter pilot more interested in war stories than Bible stories. He also teaches PE. Ruthlessly.

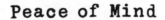

Peace of Mind

So whatever your parental requirements or security clearance, you can rest assured that Thunder Raker Manor will provide a first-class education for your child in every respect. We can't tell you how much the children enjoy being here. No, really — we can't. It's an official secret.

Chapter I

Every day, Alfie's dad went to school. But he wasn't a teacher and he didn't go there to learn Maths or study History.

No, Alfie's dad went to Thunder Raker Manor School to deliver the post. That was how Alfie got to go to the school in the first place – his dad saw it when he was doing his rounds and thought it would be just the place for his son.

It took Alfie a few days to settle in, but soon

he thought it was just the place too. Which was strange because it wasn't like any other school Alfie had ever been to or heard about: everyone who went to Thunder Raker had parents or close relatives who worked in the Secret Service or as Special Agents.

Alfie was in Class 3D, taught by Miss Jones. There were three other boys and three girls in the small class. Jack's dad was head of the Secret Service and Harry's dad had infiltrated the dastardly SPUD organisation. Sam's mum worked for Hush Hush and had built him his special gadget-laden wheelchair.

Chloe's mum was an ace spy and Alice's dad was a double agent. Or maybe a triple agent – it got a bit confusing. Beth's dad was in charge of the Government's Inventing Taskforce –

known as GIT for short.

And Alfie's dad was
the local postman.
The other children
thought this was
fantastic. How cool
that Alfie's dad had
such a great secret
identity! But Alfie
knew the real secret:
his dad *was* the local

postman. It was all a mix-up and Alfie
shouldn't really be at Thunder Raker Manor
at all. But at a school where you were
taught how to keep secrets (and how to read
codes, keep watch, disguise yourself as a
garden shed and sabotage dangerous enemy

wheelbarrows) he thought he could get away with it…

Usually Alfie was excited about going to school. But this week his class had their SATS exams. Alfie wasn't worried about the exams… well, not really. But he knew he needed to do his best. The Special Agent Training Standards were really important – if you didn't pass, you couldn't go on to take your GCSEs. And where would you be without the General Classification in Surveillance and Endurance? Well, you'd be in the same place probably. But you wouldn't be a spy.

Alfie was determined to pass first time. He'd revised all the longest rivers in the world, the date of the Spanish Armada and how to blow up secret weapons factories. He just hoped he could remember it all.

By the time Alfie walked to school, it was getting light. As he walked past old Mrs Prendergast's cottage, he saw her standing outside holding a tray of teacups. Mrs Prendergast liked making cups of tea. She took pity on the SPUD agents whose job it was to keep watch on the school, and provided them with tea and biscuits when they took their breaks.

"I saw your dad come by with the post earlier," Mrs Prendergast told Alfie, offering him a rich tea finger. "He must get up very early. I didn't even have the kettle on."

Alfie's reply was drowned out by the sound of an armoured tank as it roared past. He recognised it at once – it belonged to one of the Sixth Formers.

Mrs Prendergast was not amused. "Nasty, smelly thing," she complained. "It'll make the tea taste of oil."

Unlike the tank, the huge stretch limo that purred past Alfie made almost no noise. He only noticed it when it beeped its horn for him to move out of the way. Alfie could see Chloe's face pressed up against the darkened glass as it went past. Alfie waved and smiled, but Chloe just glared. She didn't seem to like Alfie much. The limo was bright pink.

Next to pass Alfie was a girl on a scooter. It was a push-along scooter with little tiny wheels. But welded on the back was a large jet motor and the girl was wearing a yellow crash helmet.

"Hi, Beth!" shouted Alfie above the *whoosh* of the engine as it sped erratically towards him. He moved to the left, but the scooter moved the same way – heading straight for him. Alfie jumped to the right – just as the scooter lunged that way too.

"No brakes!" Beth shouted as she screamed past. She narrowly missed Alfie and zigzagged her way towards the school gates up ahead.

The uniformed figure of Sergeant Custer, the school's security guard, leaped out from his hut beside the armoured metal gates. He dragged them open just in time for Beth's scooter to hurtle through.

As Alfie approached, Sergeant Custer saluted and smiled. "Morning, Alfie."

"Good morning, Sergeant Custer."

Alfie was just walking past the gates when the noise started. It was so sudden and so loud it made him jump. It was louder than the tank and Beth's scooter put together.

"Woof! Woof!"

Alfie backed away. An enormous guard dog

was straining at a lead tied to Sergeant Custer's hut, struggling to break free. It snarled and barked and snapped its huge jaws.

"Oy – quieten down!" Custer shouted at the

dog. "It's just because he likes you," he assured Alfie.

"Right..." Alfie wasn't convinced. He watched while Sergeant Custer calmed the dog down and managed to wrestle it back inside the hut.

"Sorry about that," panted Custer as he staggered out again, "but he's new to the team. Got to be a bit careful. He's a savage beast, trained to take out the enemy like that: *wham*!" Custer demonstrated with a punch in the air. "Or rather, *snap*! Have your arm off as soon as look at you if he thinks you're on the wrong side."

"The wrong side of what?" asked Alfie.

Custer shrugged. "Don't know. Didn't ask. These gates maybe? But you're inside now, so you should be safe from the fierce, highly trained killer guard dog."

"That's good," said Alfie. "What's his name?"

Sergeant Custer grinned with pride. "Gerald," he said fondly.

The other children were already in their seats when Alfie arrived. Usually they were racing round and having fun, so Alfie guessed they were a bit nervous about the SATS exams too. Sam had his wheelchair close to his desk. The arms of the chair opened to reveal an impressive collection of pens, pencils, sharpeners, rulers, erasers and a small can of oil.

"For the exams," he explained.

Alfie frowned. "We need *oil* for the exams? I haven't got any."

Oh no, he thought. *I haven't even started and I've already failed by not bringing the right equipment...*

"No. One of my wheels gets squeaky," explained Sam. Alfie breathed a sigh of relief.

"Don't be nervous," said Jack. "I've arranged a code with Sam so we can tell each other the answers by flashing torches."

"That's cheating," declared Alice. "Anyway Miss Jones will see you."

"She won't see me," Sam said. "I forgot my torch."

"Are the tests hard?" Alfie asked, slightly nervously.

Chloe laughed. "They're Level 3 SATS. Course they're hard."

"Don't worry," said Beth. "They won't be that difficult."

"Not for me they won't," declared Chloe. "My dad got me a Teach Yourself SATS program for my GameStation X. It's called SATS In Lessons Learned Yourself."

Alfie worked out the initial letters. "SATSILLY," he said.

"Not as silly as *you*," said Chloe crossly.

"I didn't mean…" began Alfie, but Chloe had turned her back on him in a huff.

Good one, Alfie, he thought. *As if she doesn't hate you enough already…*

Just then, Miss Jones arrived. Their class teacher was holding a bundle of plain brown envelopes.

"Right, I have your test papers here for the Special Agent Training Standards," she said. "Each of you will be given a different paper specially chosen to test how you are getting on."

"Bet mine's the hardest," Jack said.

"Not as difficult as mine," sniffed Chloe.

"Everyone's is equally difficult," Miss Jones said as she handed them out. "Just different sorts of difficult, depending on what you're good at."

When everyone had a brown envelope, a pad of paper and a pen on the desk in front of them, Miss Jones told them they had one hour to do their best. "You should do the test in silence. If there's anything you need to ask, you can put your hand up, but it really must be an emergency, something completely extraordinary that you genuinely can't deal with yourself."

The children opened the envelopes and took out their papers. They stared at them, puzzled. Then Harry grabbed his pen and started to write frantically. The others all raised their hands.

34

Chapter 2

Miss Jones sent for Mr Trenchard, the Head Teacher. Five minutes later, he was standing in front of Class 3D. None of them had even begun their SATS, apart from Harry, who was still scribbling away feverishly.

"What's wrong?" Mr Trenchard asked Miss Jones. "Why aren't they writing? Slightly thick, are they?"

Miss Jones explained the problem: when the class had opened their envelopes, the papers they found inside were not their exam papers at all. "Without the proper question papers," she concluded, "Class 3D can't possibly do their SATS."

"Sorry," Mr Trenchard said when she had finished. "Got a terrible memory. Trained myself to forget things you know. Can't quite remember why, but it did seem very useful at the time. Now, what was it you were going to tell me?"

"You can't expect me to answer this!" said Chloe indignantly, waving her exam paper. "It's an advert for a holiday on a cruise ship."

"I've got a leaflet about washing machines," said Jack.

"Any good?" Beth asked.

"Not really. No drier. What did you have?"

Beth sniffed. "Chance to win a laptop computer. Except it's a rubbish one." She turned to Alfie. "What about you?"

Alfie held up the paper that had been inside his envelope. "It seems to be a form to fill in if I want someone to send me a different saucepan each month." He checked the details. "You can collect a matching set of twenty. Non-stick."

"Who'd want saucepans?" Jack wondered.

"I've won second prize in a beauty contest," said Alice.

"Well, that's good," said Sam.

She glared at him. "*Second* prize?"

"I came first," said Sam. "Only kidding," he added quickly, as Alice opened her mouth, looking cross. "Actually I got a postcard from Aunt Tabitha." He paused. "Only I don't have an Aunt Tabitha."

"This Tabitha woman is clearly behind it all," Mr Trenchard decided. "We must track her down."

"The postcard's from Holloway Prison," Sam said. "Aunt Tabitha wants us to post her a cake. With a file inside."

"Ah, a top-secret file!" exclaimed Mr Trenchard.

"Now we're getting somewhere!"

Miss Jones sighed. "I don't think it's that sort of file," she said wearily.

But Mr Trenchard was looking round the room. His eyes settled on Harry, still leaning over his desk. "Why is that boy writing?"

"What are you doing, Harry?" Miss Jones asked.

Harry looked up, surprised. "I'm doing my test," he said. "It's really good. Not nearly as difficult as I was expecting. I just have to fill in my name and address and if I get it right, they send me matching saucepans."

The SATS weren't completely ruined though. As well as the written tests, there was also a field trip during which students could earn points towards their qualification.

"So all is not lost!" said Mr Trenchard. "I've got the trip all arranged and I'm just waiting for final permission. I've sent off the booking form for the special assault course at the British Army Training Site. As long as the Risk Assessment is OK, we'll be going BATS next week. But for now, I think you'd better carry on with your normal lessons."

Alfie wasn't sure any of his lessons were "normal". But he and the others set off for their Surveillance class with Mrs Nuffink.

As soon as they were settled, Mrs Nuffink announced, "Today we are going to be learning how to write Field Reports."

"Like farmers do?" asked Sam.

"Do we have to count daisies?" Alice wondered.

"Or maybe identify different types of grass through an electron scanning microscope," suggested Beth.

"I've got one of those," said Chloe smugly.

"Field Reports," said Mrs Nuffink loudly, "are what agents send back, describing what they have observed. I have one here that has just arrived from a very good agent who keeps watch for me on the car park at the back of the bank." She held up a large envelope.

"Cool!" said Jack. "Does he keep a lookout for gangsters?"

"Are you expecting a robbery?" asked Alfie.

"No," said Mrs Nuffink. "He lets me know

when there's a parking space. It's also handy for the greengrocer."

She opened the envelope and stared open-mouthed at the sheet of paper inside. "Congratulations," she read out. "You have won third prize in a beauty contest." She looked round the class. "Do any of you know anything about this?"

"Yeah," said Alice proudly. "I know I came second."

It was Tracking Skills next, and as usual there was a note taped to the classroom door.

"The class has moved again," Sam complained. "I wish Sir Westerly Compass would work out where we should be and stick to it."

Alfie took down the note. It was inside a plain white envelope marked '3D'. He opened it.

"So, where are we off to now?" Jack asked.

"The beautiful sun-drenched beaches of Florida," read Alfie. "Flights and luxury hotel accommodation are all included in this bargain price. Apparently."

Makes a change from Room 11F, thought Harry.

But before they could discuss it further, Beth gave a shout of warning and they all flattened themselves against the wall of the corridor. Miss Fortune – teacher of Assassination Techniques – was coming.

Sam's wheelchair crunched up so it became narrower and everyone held their breath as the kindly looking little old lady with grey hair walked past. She paused alongside Chloe and glared at her. Chloe tensed, ready to fling herself out of the way.

But Miss Fortune moved on. As she reached Alfie, she noticed the envelope he was holding. "*Knitting*?!" she screamed suddenly, like a ferocious war cry. Her right hand slammed out and Alfie ducked just in time. He leaped to one side as Miss Fortune's armoured shoe smashed into the wall behind him.

"*Knitting*?!" she shrieked again. Then she nodded politely to Sam and Alice, and continued calmly on her way.

"What was that all about?" breathed Jack.

"Something's needled her," Beth decided. "But what?"

They got their answer in Code Breaking lesson. Alfie found this subject very difficult because no one could understand what Mr Cryption said. As Class 3D arrived, he was showing an envelope to the Major, who taught Sabotage Training.

"Carpet tiles Shakespeare identity crisis talks," Mr Cryption said. He didn't sound happy and took a sheet of paper out of the envelope. He read it out: "Are you skinny? Do you have sand kicked in your face? Mrs Muscle's Bodybuilding Class could be just the thing for you."

"Doesn't make much sense, does it?" the Major sympathised. He leaned on the edge of Mr Cryption's desk to look at the paper more closely. The desk collapsed.

"Sorry," said the Major, taking a step back. Behind him, the whiteboard slipped to one side and swayed precariously. Marker pens slipped from the shelf under the board and clattered to the floor. The Major bent to pick them up and his head crashed into Mr Cryption's stomach.

"*Oof*!" gasped Mr Cryption as the wind was knocked out of him. "Artichoke wobble slingshot bananas."

The Major put the pens back on the shelf. The shelf fell off. The board followed soon after. "Miss Fortune was telling me that her

application to join Assassins Anonymous came back with a certificate saying she is now a full member of the St Swithin's Ladies' Guild of Knitting." The Major grimaced. "She wasn't very amused. I can still feel the bruises."

"Has everyone had strange post?" asked Alfie.

The Major turned to answer, knocking Mr Cryption backwards. "Heard about your test papers," he said. "Some rum goings-on for sure. Mr Trick had a new camouflage net delivered and it's a bright pink duvet. Can't hide from SPUD under that."

"Safety office binoculars pest," complained Mr Cryption. "Quibble golf zero impostor."

"Quite," the Major agreed.

"Has anything happened to you, Major?"

asked Jack as the Major turned to leave.

"Stuff's always happening to him," muttered Beth.

"I did get a letter today," the Major admitted. "Plain white envelope postmarked Oxford."

"What was in it?" asked Alfie.

The Major paused in the doorway. "Don't know. Before I could open the thing, it exploded." He smiled and walked quickly from the classroom, carefully closing the door behind him.

The door wobbled on its hinges. And fell off.

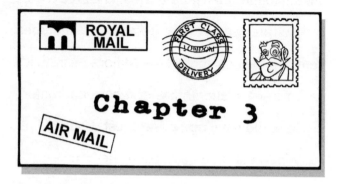

Chapter 3

"There's definitely something going wrong with the post," Alfie said at lunchtime as he sat with the boys from 3D.

They waited while the Major tripped past, Alfie leaning to one side to avoid getting the Major's drink splashed all down his back. Sam pressed a switch and a small shelf unfolded from the arm of his wheelchair to catch the Major's baked beans.

"Oops, sorry!" the Major said, but he was

talking to the small girl he'd just knocked flying.

Sam pressed another button and the shelf trembled then catapulted the Major's beans back up on to his plate. Or rather where the Major's plate should have been – he'd just dropped it as he helped the little girl back to her feet.

"Don't think that was me," the Major said, wiping baked beans and tomato sauce off the girl's face. "Er, was it?"

"My dad might know what's going wrong with the post," Alfie said once everything had calmed down.

"Oh, yes," Jack remembered. "He's infiltrated the Post Office, hasn't he?"

"Well… he works there."

"Ah, of course," said Jack, tapping the side of his nose.

"My dad's infiltrated SPUD," said Harry.

"You're not supposed to tell us that," Sam reminded him.

"I know. I just thought…" Harry was staring off into space. "I write him letters, and every two weeks he writes me one back. He sends it to the school so it can't get intercepted by SPUD. But now the letters are getting muddled up. What if SPUD find Dad's letter…?"

Alfie could see what Harry was getting at. "Yes… If SPUD get hold of your dad's letters, they'll work out he's spying on them."

"My dad doesn't spy on letters," Harry said.

"No, I mean SPUD."

"Yeah," said Harry. "And that's not all. My dad's instructions are sent from the school – who to spy on, that sort of thing. If SPUD got hold of those, he'd be in real trouble."

"So what do we do?" asked Sam. Everyone looked at Alfie.

"First we have to be sure that there really is a problem with the post and letters getting muddled. If there is, we need to find a way to visit the Sorting Office and see what's going wrong."

"And we need to get out of here fast..." added Jack.

"Why?" Alfie asked.

"Miss Fortune's just finished her lunch!"

They made it to the door just before a fork embedded itself in the wall close by.

Seconds later, a dinner plate spun across the room and sliced into a table – close to where a small girl with baked beans in her hair was nervously finishing her meal.

"That *definitely* wasn't me," the Major assured her.

*

Straight after lunch was PE. Because it was a cold, wet day, Class 3D was in the school hall.

"Right, relay races," the Chaplain announced.

"That shouldn't be too dangerous," said Alfie.

"You have *so* much to learn," sighed Chloe.

"Two teams," the Chaplain was explaining. "Run down the hall, touch the wall at the end, then back again and hand over the baton."

"That isn't a baton," Beth pointed out. "It's a hand-grenade."

"Beggars can't be choosers," said the Chaplain. "Just be careful not to nudge this pin as you climb over the barbed wire."

"Just the barbed wire?" asked Jack suspiciously.

"Well," the Chaplain conceded, "there are

concealed landmines of course. And I shall be operating the smoke machine."

"Smoke machine?" repeated Sam. "I might crash!"

"Always that risk," the Chaplain admitted. "But if you get lost, listen out for the barking."

"Er…?" said Harry. "Sorry?"

"Sergeant Custer's lent us his new guard dog for the afternoon. But I'll let the first runners get a good head start before I release him. Now, any questions?"

Alfie had one. "Did you get any post this morning, Chaplain?"

"Good one," Jack murmured. "This'll give us some more evidence."

"I did," said the Chaplain. "I was expecting the latest newsletter from the Fighter Aircraft

Tactical Solutions Organisation."

"FATSO," said Beth.

"Actually I'm in very good shape for a PE teacher," said the Chaplain indignantly. "Anyway, instead I got an appointment at Miss Pamper's Health Spa Emporium to be wrapped in seaweed for an hour and then have the hair removed from my legs with hot wax – for next Tuesday morning."

"That must have been a shock," said Alfie.

"Bit of a surprise," the Chaplain admitted as he passed Alfie a hand-grenade. "I usually have it done on a Wednesday."

"You ought to talk to Mr Trenchard about your dad," Alice told Harry. "He'll know what to do."

"If he knows who you are," said Beth. She

was helping Jack to straighten one of Sam's wheels. There was a dent in it roughly the size and shape of a guard dog's head.

"PE wasn't so bad this week," said Jack.

Chloe glared at him. "Not until the Chaplain made it a beat-the-clock race by pulling the pins out of the hand-grenades."

"At least Harry put them all back in again at the end," Alfie said.

"Er…" said Harry. "I thought Sam was doing that."

There was the *crump* of a small explosion from somewhere in the area of the school hall. Followed shortly by a roar of anger.

Harry gulped. "Let's go before he catches us."

"Right," said Alfie. "We'll go and see Mr Trenchard."

Mr Trenchard assured Harry and Alfie that of course he knew who they were. "How could I forget you, Alex?" he told Alfie. "Or you, for that matter, young Harvey."Alfie sighed. Not a good start.

Mr Trenchard held up a hand. "Just wait a moment while I finish up some paperwork."

As he waited, Alfie glanced down at a piece of paper on Mr Trenchard's desk. It was covered with files, but he could make out the top half. It was headed: *School Trip – Risk Assessment Form*. Under that was written: *Class 3D Assessment Field Trip*.

Alfie quite liked the idea of the field trip. It sounded like it might be fun. It was hard to read the paper upside-down, but Alfie managed to make out a few lines. *Third Form Field Trip for SATS. Risk = low. That is, lowish.*

Alfie swallowed and read on further: *That is, we lost three pupils last year.* Maybe the field trip wouldn't be such fun.

And Mr Phelps. Alfie gulped. Maybe Mr Trenchard wouldn't be much help after all...

But just then the Head Teacher looked up. "Right. Why are you here?" It took a few minutes for Alfie and Harry to explain.

"I see. Yes, a very serious matter," said Mr Trenchard. "And of course I am fully aware of your father's situation, Henry. Sorry – Harry. But while there has indeed been a bit of a mix-up today with the post that's been delivered I can guarantee that the mail we've been sending out won't have been affected. You're in 3D, aren't you?" he asked suddenly.

"Yes, sir," chorused Alfie and Harry.

"That reminds me, I haven't had the authorisation and booking confirmation for your SATS field trip yet." Mr Trenchard pulled the form towards him with one hand and reached for his telephone with the other. "I'll just phone and check."

Alfie and Harry were about to leave but Mr Trenchard was still talking to them as he waited for an answer to his phone call.

"There's no need to worry, Harry. I'm absolutely sure that no post sent out from this school can possibly have gone astray." He

broke off to speak into the phone: "Ah, yes –
Trenchard here. Just chasing up that form I sent
you the other day. It was in a red envelope
marked *Urgent* and *Most Secret*. Got it? Good."

Mr Trenchard covered the phone and said to
Harry, "You see. No problems. Nothing to
worry about." Harry smiled at Alfie and they
turned to go. Behind them Mr Trenchard said,
"Yes, that's the one. That's from me."

"Sounds like everything will be all right," said Harry quietly.

Then Mr Trenchard thundered, "What do you mean you don't collect saucepans?!" A few moments later, he slammed down the phone. "Right," he announced to Alfie and Harry. "It seems we have a problem with the post. And since you are now short of a SATS field trip, I'm handing this over to Class 3D to find out what's going on. Solve the case of the missing post and I'll give you full credits towards your SATS."

Chapter 4

Miss Jones thought that Alfie's suggestion was a very good one. In fact only Chloe didn't seem happy about it.

"An afternoon in a Sorting Office?" she snorted. "How boring is that?"

"Mr Trenchard suggested it really," said Harry. "And it sounds like fun to me."

"Everything sounds like fun to you," Alice told him. "Even filling in saucepan forms."

Harry frowned. "I wonder when the first one will turn up."

"The way the post is working," said Jack, "there'll be a mix-up and you'll get a cheese grater."

Harry's frown became a grin. "Do you really think so?"

"Great," Chloe muttered.

"Yes, I would," said Harry. "I'd grate cheese, carrots, everything."

"No, I mean…" Chloe turned away. "Never mind."

"I'll ask my dad this evening," said Alfie. "I'm sure he can arrange it for us."

Harry was staring open-mouthed at Alfie. "Your dad's involved with kitchen equipment?"

"He means the trip to the Sorting Office,"

Jack explained. "Not your saucepans and grater."

"While we're there, we can investigate the missing post," said Alfie.

"I'll build a detector," announced Beth. "A missing post detector."

"How will that work?" asked Sam.

"Well, we get someone to describe a letter that has gone missing. Then we draw a picture of it."

"I'll do that," said Chloe. "I'm the best at drawing."

"Then what?" asked Jack.

"Then we take all the letters we find at the Sorting Office and scan them into a computer.

And we also scan in Chloe's drawing. Then I'll write a computer program that can compare the drawing with every letter we've scanned in until it finds one that looks the same."

"If Chloe's drawing is any good," said Alice.

"And if they let us scan in all the letters," added Jack.

"In case they don't," said Beth proudly, "I have designed this." She unrolled a large piece of paper and everyone crowded round to look. It was a drawing of a boy in a wheelchair.

"That's me," said Sam.

"Right." Beth pointed to the seat of the wheelchair. "I've built a scanner underneath the seat. All Sam has to do is roll over the post and the scanner will do the rest."

"Won't anyone notice?" asked Alfie.

"Well," said Beth, "we'll have to get them to spread the letters on the floor."

"We could pretend to drop them," suggested Jack.

"And there will be a bright light shining from Sam's bottom."

"I beg your pardon?" said Harry.

"From the scanner," Alice told him.

"How long will it take?" asked Jack.

"Not long," said Beth. "About a minute to scan each letter."

"How many letters are there in a Sorting Office?" asked Sam.

"Thousands," replied Alfie.

"Oh," said Beth.

"Maybe tens of thousands."

"Oh," said Beth.

"And then there are all the letters that have already been sent out. We can't scan those."

"Oh," said Beth.

"Beth," said Sam, "what letter comes after N?"

"Funny boy," said Beth.

"Maybe we need a quicker scanner," suggested Jack.

"Or maybe," said Alfie, "we can just look for the missing letters ourselves."

Alfie had a letter from Mr Trenchard officially asking if Class 3D could visit the Sorting Office.

Alfie had persuaded Mr Trenchard to let him take it home himself and give it to his dad rather than post it.

"Otherwise we might end up looking round a saucepan factory," he said. But Mr Trenchard didn't seem to find that funny.

"I'm glad that your friends and teachers are taking such an interest," Alfie's dad said when he read the letter.

"Do you have any homework?" asked Alfie's mum.

"Just some coding and decoding for Mr Cryption." Alfie showed her the photocopied page he had to work on. It said, "Zebra bath anthology in frosting casement of violin flippers."

"And you have to decode that so it makes sense?" asked Mum.

"Oh, no," said Alfie. "That's for me to put *into* code, so people won't understand it."

"Shouldn't take long," said Dad.

The Sorting Office was like a big shed full of bags of letters and crates of parcels. Postmen and women moved the letters from one bag to another, and shifted the parcels between crates. Down the middle of the building was a large wooden frame with shelves for each street and road and avenue in the area. Letters and parcels for each were put on the correct shelf before being taken away and delivered.

"It's not what I was expecting," Beth told Alfie's dad. "Where are the robot arms to move the parcels around? Where's the high-tech scanning equipment to read postcodes and automatically sort the letters?"

"No robot arms," Alfie's dad explained. "That's done by Jim Callaghan. And no scanning equipment, unless it's Mr MacMillan's eyes." He frowned. "Children usually ask how many letters we get and what's the biggest parcel we've ever had and stuff like that."

"Thank you so much for showing us round," Miss Jones said quickly. "The children are fascinated."

"Bit boring," yawned Alice.

"When can we go?" whined Chloe.

"This is great," said Harry. "How many letters do you get? What's the biggest parcel that's ever been delivered? There's just so much post!"

"That's sort of the point," explained the Major. He was helping on the trip and Miss

Jones had asked him politely not to touch anything. "Look – this parcel is marked *Fragile*," he said. "Oops – sorry."

"That's OK. I'll get Anthony Eden to sweep it up," said Alfie's dad.

"*This Way Up*," the Major read on another parcel. "So what happens if…" There was the sound of breaking crockery.

"Ah. Can he sweep this up as well?"

Sam was whizzing backwards and forwards over any letters that were lying on the floor. "Just practising," he told Alfie.

Beth grinned. "I'm working on a quicker scanner," she explained. "Problem is, it's a bit big to go under Sam's chair so he'll need bigger wheels."

"That's fine. How big?" Sam asked.

"Might need to take them off a big digger."

Sam thought about this. "Cool," he said. "Can I have that shovel thing off the front too?"

Alfie's dad was nearing the end of the tour. He paused to steady a stack of parcels the Major had brushed past and asked, "So, does anyone have any questions? Anything at all about delivering your post?"

Alice's hand shot up. "I want to know," she said, "why I didn't get a birthday card from Aunt Geraldine last year."

"And I'd like to know," said the Major, "if all your parcels leak engine oil like this one."

Miss Jones persuaded the Major to put the soggy parcel back on the shelf where he had found it. Then several other people rushed to try to put the shelves back together again and stop the whole lot collapsing.

"I have a question," said Alfie. "Where does the post for Thunder Raker Manor go?"

"Now that's a very good question," said Miss Jones. "We have a special delivery, don't we?"

"Very special," Alfie's dad agreed. "Particularly for a school."

"I bet that's where all the gadgets and

technology come in," said Beth. "I bet the post is sorted by a computer that automatically reads the addresses, then it goes on to a special shelf that tips up and slides it down a chute into a scanner so everything is double-checked. Then it gets neatly stacked by robot arms in a big container that is security sealed ready for delivery."

"It's a bit like that," Alfie's dad admitted. He pointed to a postbag leaning against the wall nearby. "Actually Winston puts it all in that sack."

"And does it just get left there?" asked Alfie. "Where anyone can see it?" He walked over and examined the sack of post.

"Oh, no," his dad explained, quickly steering the Major past a foam-filled fire extinguisher.

"Because it's special it gets locked in the back of the van when we close up the Sorting Office. And then I check again that I've got the right post before I deliver it to Thunder Raker Manor in the morning."

"Oops – sorry," said the Major as the Sorting Office began to fill with foam. "I think that might have been me."

Chapter 5

It was a wet break that afternoon, so Class 3D were indoors.

"That visit was a complete waste of time," said Chloe. "I blame Alfie. He arranged it."

"I thought it was very interesting," said Alice. "I shall tell Aunt Geraldine."

"But we're no closer to knowing what's happening to the post," Beth pointed out. "And Harry's dad will be sending him a letter in a couple of days. There's no way we can stop it –

we can't even write to him."

"We know it gets *sorted* properly," said Alfie. "So the problem must be after it leaves the Sorting Office."

"How do we know that?" demanded Chloe.

"Because I looked in the sack," said Alfie. "And it was full of post addressed to Thunder Raker. It didn't look like it had been opened. But to be absolutely sure I slipped in a letter addressed to Class 3D. So we can see if it gets delivered and if so, whether it's been tampered with."

"Is this it?" asked Alice. She picked up a letter that had been left on Miss Jones's desk.

"Yes," Alfie said. "Let's see what's inside. It should just be a note saying 'This is a test, by Alfie'."

Alice opened the envelope and took out a sheet of paper. "Almost right," she said. "Apparently our subscription to *Cauliflower and Broccoli News* is about to expire and we can get a great deal if we renew it now."

"That proves that the problem is between the Sorting Office and Thunder Raker," said Jack. "Which is good because I've developed this plan." He turned to Sam. "Show time." The arm of Sam's wheelchair opened and a mini-projector rose from inside. It angled towards the class whiteboard and a picture appeared.

"Pigeons," announced Jack proudly. There was silence for a while as everyone looked at the picture of a pigeon projected on the board.

"Definitely a pigeon," agreed Alice.

"What about pigeons?" asked Harry.

"Not just ordinary pigeons, but THPs," Jack said.

"Terribly Helpful Pigeons?" asked Alice.

"Ten Horrible Pigeons?" suggested Chloe.

"Three Heroic Pigs," said Harry. "Er, in disguise," he added.

Jack sighed. "Trained Homing Pigeons," he said. "Obviously."

Sam worked a control and the picture of the pigeon was replaced by a map of the area. In the middle of the map was some writing.

"SOX," Alfie read out loud.

"Do pigeons wear socks?" asked Harry.

"It doesn't say socks," Jack told them. "Look – SO."

There was a pause. "So – what?" asked Alice.

"What do you mean, so what? It's obvious," retorted Jack.

"You're losing me," confessed Sam. "What does SOX mean if it isn't socks?"

"It doesn't say socks or SOX," said Jack, frustrated. "It says SO. Stands for Sorting Office. And the X marks where it is. And these arrows," he went on quickly, waving at Sam to display the next picture, "show how the pigeons get there."

Arrows appeared across the map, all coming from different directions, but all ending up at the X of SOX.

"And what do these pigeons do?" Chloe wanted to know.

"They keep watch," explained Jack. "They home in on the letters, follow them and report

back what happens."

"How do the pigeons know which letters are for Thunder Raker Manor?" asked Alfie.

"I told you, they're trained."

"Trained to read?" frowned Beth.

"And how," Alfie wondered, "do they report back to us?"

"They're homing pigeons. Once they see

what's going on, they'll come *home*."

"And then what?" asked Sam. "I mean, they can't tell us what they saw, can they?" Jack didn't answer. "Can they?" repeated Sam.

"Cameras," said Jack. "We fit them with special cameras."

"And train them to use these cameras," smirked Chloe. "After we've taught them to read..."

"Who's going to teach them to read?" wondered Alice.

"Not Jack," said Harry, peering at the map. "Look – he can't spell 'socks'."

"How about we use badgers instead?" suggested Jack.

"How about," said Beth, "we use *my* plan." She held up a chunky mobile phone.

"You're going to phone the pigeons?" said Harry.

"Badgers," Jack corrected him. "Keep up, Harry. And they could text us actually."

"Do badgers have thumbs?" Alfie wondered.

"Can they spell?" asked Chloe.

"Don't need to for texting," said Sam. "It's all like LOL and CU and RU OK."

"And SOX," added Alice.

Beth cleared her throat. "No pigeons. No badgers. Just this special phone."

"So tell us what's special about it," said Alfie.

"GPS," said Beth.

"Guinea Pig Shaped," said Sam knowingly.

"Global Positioning System," Beth corrected him. "It means the phone knows exactly where it is at all times."

"How does that help?" asked Jack.

"We post the phone," said Beth. "Package it up and send it to ourselves here."

"And then what?" asked Chloe.

"This phone has a built-in timer," Beth told them. "I'll set it for this time tomorrow. By then the parcel should have been intercepted and gone astray."

"And we'll know where it is," Jack realised. "Brilliant. That's brilliant. We can send the badgers to get it back."

"What do you think, Alfie?" asked Sam.

"It's a good plan," said Alfie. "But I can't help feeling we're missing something."

"Just because it wasn't your idea," sneered Chloe. "I think it's great. What can go wrong?"

The next afternoon, they found out.

At exactly the time Beth had set on the phone's timer, they all gathered in Classroom 3D. Beth had another mobile phone, which she had wired to the speakers built in to the headrest on Sam's wheelchair.

"Just about now," she announced.

A blast of sound echoed round the room. Sam's cheeks wobbled and his jaw dropped open. His hair seemed to be standing on end as the ring tone erupted from the speakers close to his head.

"I'll just turn it down a bit!" Beth shouted over the noise. "Right, here we go." She held up the phone so they could all see and pressed the receive call button. There was silence.

"I think you turned it down too far," said Alice.

"Hello?" Jack shouted close to Sam's ear, making him flinch. "Hello? Anyone there? Can you hear me? WHERE – ARE – YOU?"

"I knew there was something we missed," said Alfie quietly. "The phone just called us, right?"

"Yes," said Beth proudly.

"The phone that knows exactly where it is," continued Alfie.

"Yes."

"So that we can trace where the post is going missing."

"Yes."

"So," said Jack, realising what Alfie meant, "how does the phone *tell us* where it is?"

There was a pause. Then Beth said, "Well, I can't think of *everything*."

There was silence for a while, broken only by the distant sound of a dog barking. "I think that dog's on the phone," said Alfie.

"Dogs don't use phones," Alice told him. "Anyway, who would it call?"

"No, I mean it's at the other end. Where the phone is. Where our post is."

"That's it then," said Sam. "We train the dog. Teach it to bark in code or something. Then it can tell us where it lives."

"I'm sorry," said Chloe, "are you suggesting we train a dog down the phone? That's just daft." She shook her head sadly. "It's much easier over the internet."

"I've got a plan," said Harry. Everyone looked at him in surprise.

"I have. Really. I know how we can find out where the phone is and what's happened to all our letters and parcels."

"So what *is* your plan?" asked Sam.

Harry smiled. "We post Alfie."

Chapter 6

Alfie was not convinced, but since he didn't have another plan and everyone thought he was the best person for the mission, he eventually agreed. That evening, after school, he explained to his mum and dad that he was going to be staying at school the following night.

"It's a sort of special project. For our SATs exams."

"That's nice, Alfie," his mum said. "They will

give you tea, won't they?"

"I expect so."

"Do you need a sleeping bag or anything?"
Dad asked.

"I think it's all provided," said Alfie.

"Better take a toothbrush anyway," Mum told
him. "And a clean pair of pants."

The next afternoon, Alfie was parcelled up in a
box marked *Thunder Raker Manner Skool –
Erjunt*. Harry had been in charge of the
labelling.

Chloe had seemed very keen to wrap Alfie
tightly in parcel tape. But Alfie had managed to
persuade everyone else that it would be better
if he was inside a big box and could move
about.

"Alfie's definitely right," said Jack. "After all, he's got to be able to move so he can train that dog."

"What?" said Alfie, stepping into an enormous cardboard box that used to contain PE equipment. On one side was written in big letters: *Flammable Material. Extreme Caution. Do Not Drop.* And there were burn marks.

"Why do I need to train the dog?" Alfie continued.

"Well, because that's the plan," said Jack. "We post you, you end up wherever the letters have gone, and then you train the dog to read the position off Beth's phone and to bark in code so it can tell us where it is."

"I still think we could have used the internet," said Chloe.

"Do you need a dog-training manual?" asked Sam.

"I don't think so," Alfie told him. "I was just going to find out where I end up and then come back and tell everyone."

There was a pause while the other children stared at Alfie. Then Alice said, "Brilliant!"

Alfie was feeling very hot as he sat down inside the box. He pulled his toothbrush out of his pocket and poked a few holes

in the side. It was still very warm and it got dark as the lid came down. He could see Beth staring down anxiously at him through the closing gap.

"You will be all right?" asked Beth quietly.

Alfie nodded. Actually he was a bit nervous – he didn't like enclosed spaces. But he didn't want to let Beth know that.

"I'll be fine," he assured her. He reached into his pocket for his hanky and wiped his hot forehead, smiling to show he was OK really.

"I think we should send him second class," Chloe was saying from behind Beth.

"So he has lots of time to find out what's going on."

"Alfie," Beth said. "Why are you wiping your face with a pair of pants?"

Yeah, thought Alfie. *Really cool. Nice one, Alfie.*

"It will look a bit suspicious if lots of us turn up at the Post Office just to send a parcel," said Beth. "We'll use Sam's prongs."

Sam's wheelchair had extendable prongs that came out from the arms to turn it into a sort of fork-lift truck. Jack and Harry managed to lift the large box containing Alfie on to them. Immediately the wheelchair fell forwards under the weight, sending Sam sprawling across the box.

"Ow!" said Sam.

"Umff!" said the box.

"Alfie's too heavy," sniffed Chloe.

"Well, he hasn't got time to go on a diet," Alice told her.

So Jack and Harry climbed on the back of Sam's wheelchair, and with their weight, it tilted upright again. Motors straining, the wheelchair rolled out of the classroom and started off down the school drive.

Chloe, Alice and Beth watched the boys reach the main gate. The wheelchair was a strange sight, with the huge box sticking out in front of it and Harry and Jack clinging desperately to the back as they picked up speed down the hill towards the Post Office.

"It'll be fine," said Beth. "Nothing suspicious there at all."

The sounds were muffled inside the box. But when Alfie pressed his face to the peepholes he'd made with his toothbrush, he could see Jack and Harry arguing about who should pay the postage, and how expensive it was to send a parcel these days.

Alfie wondered if it would help if he jumped. If he could time it so the parcel was being weighed while he was in the air then it wouldn't be so heavy. Not until he landed again anyway. But there wasn't much room for jumping, and if the box started bouncing up and down, that might attract unwanted postal attention.

Finally the box was carried again for a while by someone who kept complaining about the weight. All Alfie could see was the blue of a postman's uniform, filling his eyeholes. Then there were a strange and exciting few moments when Alfie felt almost as if he was flying. Then the box hit the ground hard, knocking Alfie over and bruising his knees, and he realised he *had* been flying.

He could hear the sounds of the Sorting Office, muffled through the thick cardboard. A little light crept in through the holes, and if he pressed his eye close to the biggest, Alfie could see the legs of the postmen as they walked past.

Alfie finally dozed off and didn't wake up again until early the next morning when he felt his box slam down hard. There was a crash of metal doors and then the revving of an engine. He could just make out the inside of the post van. Alfie took a deep breath – this was it. He was about to be delivered.

"Sign here," said a man as Alfie's box was unloaded and dumped on the ground again.

"Just pop it in here," a muffled voice replied. "I'm off on my rounds in a minute."

There was something familiar about the voice, but Alfie couldn't work out what and he couldn't see who was speaking. Then he couldn't hear any more over the sound of a dog barking and the van driving off.

It was very dark wherever Alfie was and the sound of barking grew fainter. He seemed to be in the corner of a room, his peephole facing a blank wall. Somewhere in the distance a door slammed shut. Then, before Alfie could decide what to do next, the world moved.

The box was tipping sideways. He felt himself tumbling and the view through the peephole somersaulted. Alfie landed on his side. The peephole was now on the bottom of the box and all he could see through it was a bit of floorboard.

"Look – a box!" said a deep voice urgently but quietly from just the other side of the cardboard. Alfie held his breath. What was going on?

"It's quite heavy," the voice went on. "Reckon it's important?"

The reply was a high-pitched, nasal whine. "Let's get it back to SPUD's Secret Headquarters and find out. Quick, before that monster of a dog finds us."

Alfie felt himself being lifted up and through the holes he could now see heavy boots caked in mud. Then the floor beneath them seemed to disappear into blackness and he felt himself being lowered into a deep, dark pit. Torchlight flashed round, illuminating what looked like walls made of mud and earth.

A tunnel.

Alfie's box was set down and he caught a

glimpse of a dark uniform. SPUD agents, he realised – he'd been kidnapped by SPUD agents and was being taken to some secret lair, maybe even their Headquarters.

Oh no! Alfie thought. *I'm really in trouble now.*

He began to breathe heavily with fright then forced himself to hold his breath. He didn't want the SPUD agents to hear. He bit his lip and closed his eyes tight.

Just leave the box, he thought. *Just leave it…*

"You should tell the boss," the whiny voice said quietly. "Tell him we've captured a secret enemy parcel."

Alfie strained to see what was happening. If he twisted round, he could just make out one of the two men opening a small laptop computer.

The man tapped on the keyboard for a moment and the screen flickered into life. It showed a video-link to a man sitting behind a desk.

The Head of SPUD!

Except that from inside the box, Alfie couldn't see the boss's face. All he could make out was the shape of the man's shoulders, and his white-gloved hands as he stroked a large black rat sitting on the desk in front of him. The rat's eyes gleamed darkly as if it was staring hungrily back at Alfie.

"What have you to report this time?" the man on the video-link asked. His voice was smooth and full of authority. "Ripped trousers perhaps? Teeth marks in your leg maybe?"

"We've captured a secret enemy parcel," the whiny voiced SPUD agent replied. He sounded very pleased with himself.

The white-gloved hand hesitated in mid rat-stroke. Then it resumed. "Well, that's an improvement. And what, may I ask, is in this parcel?"

"Er," Whiny-voice said. "Um."

"You haven't even opened it, have you?"

"We wanted to let you know straightaway, sir," the deeper-voiced agent replied quickly. "We're just looking now."

Alfie pressed himself into a corner of the

box as he heard the lid move. The tape holding it closed was creaking as something wriggled underneath. A hand appeared above Alfie's head, clutching inside the box. Alfie hunched over as much as possible, holding his breath.

Turn invisible! he commanded himself. If ever there was a time to develop superpowers, it was right now. Or maybe Beth could invent an invisibility beam or something. Only there was no time now.

"It's really well sealed," Deep-voice was saying. "Taped up good and proper. Must be important stuff. Let me see what I can reach."

His fingers stretched further down and Alfie searched frantically for something to push towards the hand – something that would convince the SPUD agents the box wasn't worth taking.

"Hang on," said Deep-voice. "Got something here." The hand withdrew. There was a pause. "Oh."

"Well?" the rat-stroking Head of SPUD demanded. "What is it?"

"Pants," gulped the whiny-voiced agent.

There was a pause. "I can understand your disappointment," the Head of SPUD said, "but I really don't think that sort of language is called for."

"No, sorry, sir. The box – it seems to be full of… pants. Underwear."

"What should we do with it?" asked Deep-voice a bit nervously.

"I suggest you put it back so as not to arouse suspicion and find something more useful next time." The laptop screen abruptly went dark.

Moments later, Alfie's spare pants were pushed back through the lid of the box and he felt himself being lifted again. There was a creaking noise, like a badly oiled door being opened, and his box was heaved up and slammed down again. Somewhere nearby a dog was barking, and the creaking door sound came again, then there was silence…

Deciding this was as good a time as any to

find out where he was and what was going on, Alfie pushed at the top of the box. Despite the SPUD agent's efforts, the tape holding the box shut was quite strong, so Alfie stood up as high as he could and pushed up hard with both hands. The cardboard gave way and Alfie burst through.

Only it wasn't his hands that came through the top of the box. It was his feet that came through the bottom. The box was now up to his waist, with his legs sticking out. Alfie struggled to get his hands through too, staggering backwards and forwards, bumping into things.

There was a shriek of surprise and fear from outside the box. "Blooming Nora – the post's alive!"

"No, no!" Alfie shouted quickly, trying to regain his balance.

"It can talk! It's a robot!"

"No – no – no!" yelled Alfie.

"It's a robot and its voice has got stuck so it only says *No!*"

"No," Alfie insisted, still pushing at the box. "No, no, no!"

"See what I mean!"

Finally the box came loose and Alfie staggered out of it. Just as a large dog hurtled towards him.

"Alfie?!" said a voice.

"Sergeant Custer?" said Alfie.

"Gerald!" Sergeant Custer shouted.

"Woof!!" replied Gerald.

"Woah— *Ooff!*" said Alfie.

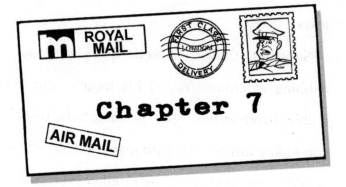

Chapter 7

It took Sergeant Custer a few minutes to get Gerald the guard dog off Alfie and tie him up outside the hut by the school's main gates. Then he came back with a mug of tea for Alfie.

"Thanks," said Alfie. "I needed that."

"Mrs Prendergast made it for me," Sergeant Custer explained. "She brings me a mug of tea just before I do my rounds each morning. I leave Gerald on guard here while I check the fences."

"Doesn't she give you any biscuits?" Alfie joked.

Sergeant Custer looked quickly away, dabbing at crumbs round his mouth with a grubby handkerchief. "So," he said, "why were you hiding inside a big cardboard box then?"

Alfie explained about the problems with the post. Sergeant Custer listened quietly. "SPUD agents, here?" he said nervously, looking round. He seemed to be slowly sinking into his chair. He wiped his perspiring face.

"Do you want to borrow mine?" asked Alfie as Sergeant Custer inspected his grubby handkerchief.

"I think I'll stick with this hanky," said Sergeant Custer. "Those are your pants."

"Sorry," said Alfie, quickly putting them back

115

in his pocket. "My mum made me bring spares. Don't know why."

"I'm afraid it's all to do with Gerald," sighed Sergeant Custer.

Alfie's mouth dropped open. "Gerald wears pants?"

Sergeant Custer stared back at Alfie. "Does he? I never noticed."

"No, I mean…" Alfie shook his head. "I don't know how the SPUD agents are involved, but I think you'd better tell me what's going on."

"Well," Sergeant Custer explained, "every day at about this time, I do my rounds. I leave Gerald on guard. And usually, while I'm out, the post arrives, though it was a bit early today. The postman leaves it in a special sealed box inside the door of the hut. He takes out the post we're sending and leaves the post that's coming in to us." Sergeant Custer pointed to a large metal box with a dial on it like a safe. "The box is over there, next to my knitting."

"That's my dad," said Alfie. "Not the knitting. Or the box," he added quickly. "I mean, my dad leaves the post."

"Good cover," agreed Sergeant Custer knowingly. "Then he has to get to his real work pretty quick, I bet. Helicopter is it?"

"He has a van sometimes."

"It started the first day I had Gerald," Sergeant Custer went on. "I got back from my rounds and found the post all over the floor. Letters and parcels all ripped open and scattered about." He shook his head sadly as he remembered.

"So what did you do?" asked Alfie.

"I didn't dare put the lights on in case anyone saw. Can't bear to think of poor Gerald getting the blame. They might even send him away, especially if SPUD's involved somehow. So I had to work in the dark, stuffing the letters and leaflets and everything back into the envelopes as best I could. I had to guess which came from where. And now it happens every day. But luckily," he said, "I don't think anyone has noticed."

"Um," said Alfie.

"Though my own post has been a bit weird recently," said Sergeant Custer. "I've been waiting to find out how Gerald and I did in a beauty contest."

"Ah," said Alfie.

"And I haven't heard from my Aunt Tabitha for ages."

"Oh," said Alfie.

"But at least they've stopped sending me those leaflets about collecting saucepans."

Miss Jones didn't seem to mind that Alfie was slightly late for school that morning, after talking to Sergeant Custer.

"That's all right, Alfie," Miss Jones said as he hurried to his desk. "And you might like to know you have parcel tape stuck to your bottom."

"It says *Other Way Up*," Sam told Alfie as he sat down. "Only kidding," he added. "Don't sit on your head."

Everyone was desperate to hear about Alfie's parcel adventure. But they had to wait until break time before they could talk.

Alfie explained about the SPUD agents who seemed to appear from nowhere and disappear again just as mysteriously. He told them about the scary SPUD boss with the pet rat. He told them about Sergeant Custer and how he thought Gerald was mixing up the post. "But with those SPUD agents about," said Alfie, "I don't think he's to blame at all. Anyway how would a dog get a special secure safety-locked postbox open?"

"Training," said Chloe confidently. "Someone trained him. Probably over the internet."

"But who trained Gerald to mix up the post?" Harry wondered.

"No one," said Alfie.

"Must have been those SPUD agents," said Jack.

"That's right," agreed Sam. "They'd want to get at our post and find out what's going on. Rotten SPUD has eyes everywhere."

"We should tell Mr Trenchard," said Beth sensibly.

"But we don't want to get Gerald into trouble," said Alice.

"When are you expecting the next letter from your dad?" Alfie asked Harry.

"Day after tomorrow," he said glumly.

"Right then," Jack announced. "We've got two days. Time for Plan B."

"Which is?" asked Alfie.

"It's what comes after Plan A," said Harry. "I

know because Jack told me that. Then you get Plan C, and after that…"

"Thank you, Harry," said Jack quickly. "Plan B is a diversionary mission in which we take GTGD into SPC and put an FGD in SCH. I suggest Sam. Any questions?"

"What does SAM stand for?" asked Alice.

"Nothing," said Jack, puzzled.

"Must stand for something."

"It's just Sam. You know." Jack pointed at Sam. "Sam."

"I stand for peace and freedom," Sam said. "Does that help? Oh, and free chocolate."

"Sorry," Alfie said, "can you tell us the plan again, but without the initials?"

Jack sighed. "It's very easy. We take GTGD, that's Gerald The Guard Dog, into SPC –

Special Protective Custody. And we put an FGD, or Fake Guard Dog, in Sergeant Custer's hut. Like I said, I suggest Sam."

"Secret Armed Militia?" asked Sam. "Or Some Actual Mongrel?"

"I think he means you," said Alfie.

"So, we disguise Sam," said Beth slowly, "as a dog?"

"Does DOG stand for anything?" Harry wondered.

"It'd be a big dog," Chloe pointed out.

"With wheels," added Alice.

"But hey," Beth told them, "I could rig up night-vision surveillance and cameras, and he could have my mobile phone."

"I like the cameras and stuff," said Sam. "But I don't think I'd make a very good dog."

"OK," Jack conceded. "Let's forget the FGD and we'll go with Beth's cameras and stuff. We wire the place, right? Miniature cameras cover every centimetre of the inside of Sergeant Custer's hut and we watch what happens and what those SPUD guys are up to."

"I guess so," said Alfie. "It sounds simpler than the fake dog."

"First," Jack went on, "we need to catch the woodpeckers. If we glue their feet to the outside wall of the hut, they'll have to keep pecking in the same place and that'll give us holes to poke the cameras through."

"Might take a while," said Beth. "Maybe we need to reinforce their beaks with titanium steel?"

"And we should snuggle up outside under that pink duvet Mr Trick had delivered for camouflage," said Harry.

"That won't disguise us very well," Chloe told him.

Harry looked puzzled. "I meant to keep warm. While the woodpeckers are making holes for the night-vision surveillance cameras."

Alfie cleared his throat. "Or," he said, "we could just watch through the window."

Chapter 8

The next morning all of Class 3D arrived at school early. Alfie had warned Sergeant Custer they were going to be keeping watch.

"I couldn't get a woodpecker," Jack whispered as they gathered at the back of the guard hut. "But maybe we can find some woodworms?"

They all crept up to the small window in the back wall of the hut. Standing on tip-toe they could see in. Except Alice who was too small and Sam who was stuck in his chair. Alice climbed up on Sam's foot supports, but that didn't help Sam.

"What's going on?" he wanted to know.

"Nothing," Chloe told him. "This is a silly idea."

There was a bang from the front of the hut. "Guns!" Harry exclaimed.

"Sergeant Custer slamming the door shut," said Alfie.

Sure enough, a few moments later they saw Sergeant Custer making his way through the grey early morning light along the perimeter fence. There was a forlorn barking from inside the hut.

"What's happening now?" asked Sam.

"Still nothing," Jack told him.

"I want to see," said Sam.

Alice gave a shriek as Sam's wheelchair lurched and wobbled, then started to rise upwards. "We're flying!" she said.

"No," explained Sam. "Hydraulic lift. Mum added it last summer so I could see properly at Sports Day. And cheat in the hurdles."

"Wasn't much to see at Sports Day," Harry grumbled. "Not after the Chaplain released the tigers."

"Shhh," Chloe warned. "I think something's happening."

They all stared into the hut. The room had been dark, but now a square of light appeared on the floor. Alfie realised it was a trapdoor opening. As he watched, two men dressed entirely in black climbed into the room.

"SPUD agents!" whispered Beth.

"From their Observation and Recovery Team, ORT," said Jack. "Dad's mentioned them. Their motto is *ORT – To Know Better.*"

"Let's see what they do," Alfie told everyone.

The two men were feeling their way carefully round the darkened room. Eventually they found the sealed box with the post in it.

"They'd find it easier," said Beth, "if they took off their sunglasses."

The two men were fiddling with the lock and soon they had the box open. They reached inside and took out handfuls of letters and packages, spreading them over the floor and sorting through them. They carefully opened the envelopes and spread out all the letters and leaflets they found inside.

"What are they looking for?" asked Harry.

"Anything secret," Alice guessed.

"But they'll just put everything else away where they found it," Sam said. "I don't see how it all gets ripped open and muddled."

Then it happened and they all saw exactly how the post got ripped open and muddled.

Maybe he heard something, or maybe he smelled something, but somehow Gerald the guard dog knew the SPUD agents were in the back room of the hut. The door burst open and a mass of hair and teeth flew at the two men in black.

Gerald's feet skidded on the letters and leaflets and the contents of the packages as he went for the SPUD agents. Soon the whole room was a blizzard of paper, parcels, teeth and shreds of black uniform.

The two men abandoned the post and hurled themselves back down through the trapdoor. The door slammed shut behind them and Gerald landed on top of it, panting hard and growling angrily.

"Gerald's not to blame at all," said Alice.

"No," agreed Chloe. "Gerald's a hero."

But Harry seemed gloomy. "I bet those ORT men are trying to find out about my dad," he said. "They know there's a double agent in SPUD and if they find Dad's letters to me, they'll know who it is."

"Don't worry," Alfie told him. "They haven't found anything yet or they wouldn't still be looking."

"But how do we stop them?" Sam wondered.

"Seal up the trapdoor," said Chloe. "Put in a

state-of-the-art anti-intruder detection and elimination system. I've got one for my wardrobe."

"Or we could trick SPUD into thinking they know all about the double agent, when in fact they've got it all wrong," said Alfie.

"And how do we do that?" Chloe demanded.

"Do you have a plan, Alfie?" asked Jack.

Alfie nodded. "Let's send SPUD a letter," he said.

Chapter 9

Mr Trenchard was very interested to hear all about what Alfie and his friends had discovered.

"You mean to tell me," he said as Class 3D explained, "that our post has been going missing and getting muddled?" He shook his head sadly. "But I got a very intriguing leaflet about saucepans only yesterday. I think it must be in code," he confided quietly. "Passed it on to Mr Cryption for analysis."

"What did he say?" asked Alfie.

"Something about hat stands and xylophones. Seemed to make sense at the time." Mr Trenchard clapped his hands together. "Right then, Alfie – tell us your plan."

"He's going to send SPUD a letter," said Chloe. "Like that'll help."

"Harry's expecting his dad's letter tomorrow," said Alfie. "I thought we should provide another letter that would interest SPUD. One that tells them something we *do* want them to think, not something we *don't* want them to find out. In other words – something that isn't true."

Mr Trenchard looked carefully at Alfie. "I like the keen thrust of your mind," he announced. "I'm turning this mission over to Class 3D at once. If things work out, you'll all get As for your SATS."

While Alfie worked on the letter, Miss Jones got all the other children to design the envelope. They used stickers that said *Classified* and a stamp that said **CONFIDENTIAL**. They addressed it carefully to *The Head of the Secret Service* and added *Eyes Only* in big letters after that.

"Of course it's eyes only," Beth grumbled. "You can't *hear* a letter."

"You can if you have the latest text-to-speech reader add-on for your PS4," Chloe told her.

"Well, you can't smell a letter," said Sam.

"You can if it's from my Uncle Oscar," Jack told him.

"Guessing you wouldn't try to taste it then,"

said Alice. "Where shall I put this *Top Secret* sticker?"

"How can a sticker be top secret?" Harry wanted to know. "I mean, you only have to look at it to see what it says."

"And what it says is *Top Secret*," Alice told him.

"That's what I mean. Here, let's have a look." Harry was disappointed to find the sticker really did say *Top Secret*. "Maybe it's scratch and sniff," he grumbled.

"Yeah," said Jack. "Uncle Oscar does those too."

Finally the envelope was finished. They proudly showed it to Alfie, who was very impressed. He put the letter he had written inside and sealed it up. Everyone looked at the finished result – with its *Top Secret* sticker, **CONFIDENTIAL** stamped across it several times, *Eyes Only* instructions and a *To Be Opened By Addressee Only* note. Sam had written across it in big red letters ***ON NO ACCOUNT TO BE OPENED BY SPUD***.

"So how do we make sure," Harry asked slowly, "that the SPUD agents know this letter is important?"

The next morning, Sergeant Custer placed Class 3D's letter on top of the newly arrived post in the sealed box. Then he announced in a loud voice, "Right, Gerald, I'm just off to check the perimeter fence exactly as usual. No change of plan today at all. I'll be back in 15 minutes, just like I always am. Oh yes." Then he set off on his walk alongside the fence. Whistling loudly.

"Nothing suspicious there," said Beth confidently to the other children as they watched from a small wooded area close to the hut.

They'd taken advice from Mrs Nuffink on surveillance techniques and rigged up a very simple camera that looked in through the hut window. Now they were all watching on a small monitor screen. If anyone glanced over to the woodland, they would see no sign of the children hidden in the green and brown of the trees.

Just a large pink duvet flapping gently in the breeze.

"At least the Major's keeping well out of it," Chloe told them. "He said he was going for a walk in the village."

"This better work," said Harry nervously. "Dad's letter will arrive today."

"I think something's happening," said Alfie, pointing at the monitor. On the screen, they could see the two black-clad figures emerging from their secret trapdoor and feeling their way round the room.

"They've found the letter!" said Beth excitedly as the SPUD agents got the box open. They were holding up the fake letter, examining it and jumping about with evident glee.

"We're not out of the woods yet," said Alfie.

"No," agreed Harry. "We're under a duvet *in* the woods."

"That isn't what Alfie meant," Sam told him. But his words were drowned out by the sound of barking.

Gerald was charging at the men in black, just as before. The SPUD agents leaped for their trapdoor, just as before. But this time, they didn't get it closed in time and Gerald leaped down after them.

Beth had to shout above the echoing sound of barks and yells. "Quick, Sam!"

"Quicksand?" Harry leaped to his feet. "Nobody move!"

"Activate your directional microphones," said Beth.

"I don't have any," said Harry. "And there's quicksand."

"We can follow the barking and see where the tunnel goes," Beth was telling Sam. "Point the microphones at the ground and find the barking."

"What is quicksand anyway?" Harry asked Alfie as they followed Sam and Beth across the lawn. Sam had a screen that showed the volume of noise he was detecting as a line of blobs. The more blobs, the louder the noise.

"Do we actually need that?" Jack shouted above the sounds of underground barking and shouts of panic.

"No," said Beth. "But it looks good."

They raced back and forth across the lawn, snaking round and doubling back on themselves as they followed the sound of barking under their feet.

"It's a rubbish tunnel," Chloe complained. "I'm waiting here." She sat down on the grass.

"You'll get left behind," Jack told her as he went past a second time.

"No, I won't," she said as Jack and the others came back again.

But then the tunnel headed straight back for the main gate, and Chloe had to jump up again and follow.

"Quick!" shouted Alfie. "We can't let Gerald catch them. They have to escape with that fake letter."

But they didn't need to worry. Out of the gate, and down the lane, the barking suddenly stopped. It was replaced by a gruff voice that echoed out of Sam's headrest speakers for them all to hear: "Was that me? Sorry."

The Major.

Ahead of them was a hole in the ground where the tunnel had caved in. Two very muddy SPUD agents struggled out and sprinted down the road. One of them had a ragged hole in the seat of his black trousers. Underneath it

he was wearing red-spotted underpants. But
Alfie was delighted to see he was still clutching
the letter.

Sitting at the bottom of the hole in the
ground was the Major. Gerald was happily
licking his face. The Major looked up at Alfie

and the others. "I was just walking along and everything sort of collapsed," he said sheepishly.

Mr Trenchard and Sergeant Custer came running up just in time to hear what the Major was saying.

"Well done, Major!" said Mr Trenchard.

"And well done, Gerald," said Sergeant Custer.

"Woof!" said Gerald.

"Er, oops," said the Major, holding up Gerald's broken collar. "Was this important?"

Chapter 10

Later that day there was a special assembly. Once Mr Trenchard had remembered why he'd asked the whole school to attend, he congratulated Class 3D on their excellent plan.

"And I can now reveal," continued Mr Trenchard, "that I have had a coded message from a certain person's father who works inside SPUD." He winked at Harry. "And it is this minute being decoded for me."

Mr Cryption was standing at the back of the

school hall, waving a piece of paper.

"Excellent," said Mr Trenchard. "Now, what does the secret message say?"

"Cardigans," Mr Cryption told them all proudly. "Doom Vikings alert sleepwalker enormous igloo nightmare."

"Did that actually almost make sense?" Alice whispered.

"It did to Mr Cryption," said Jack.

"So there you have it," Mr Trenchard announced. "The fake letter seems to have worked, and SPUD's Observation and Recovery Team have retrieved evidence that their own Supreme Head is a double agent working for us. Apparently they've already arrested him."

The Major raised a muddy hand. "Excuse me, but you said he was the Supreme Head of the Observation and Recovery Team – so would he be SHORT?"

"No idea," Mr Trenchard admitted. "I've

never seen him." He turned back to the assembled students. "Now that we've closed down the SPUD tunnel, thanks to the Major here, our letters are once again safe. Never again will we have mixed-up mail and peculiar post. Everything is back to normal and properly sorted. And in recognition of that, I have a special certificate for the children in Class 3D, who have all passed their SATS with distinction."

Mr Trenchard beckoned them all on to the stage. Alfie shook hands with him and then with Jack and Sam and Harry. He smiled at Beth and Alice. Chloe glared at him, but her lip was quivering a bit, as if she really wanted to smile.

Mr Trenchard held up an impressive-looking envelope. "For Class 3D, in recognition of their

outstanding achievement," he announced and handed it to Alfie. Alfie carefully opened the envelope and pulled out the impressive-looking certificate.

"Congratulations!" he read out in a loud, proud voice so the whole school could hear. "You have been specially selected for this unique opportunity to buy a wonderful collection of matching saucepans."

READ ON FOR LOADS OF EXTRA CONTENT

Become a Secret Agent

Use this badge to fill in your secret agent details, but remember to keep it somewhere secret (like inside your sock) or other spies might find it. You never know who's watching you!

You can copy or trace the badge, or if you have a printer, go to www.harpercollins.co.uk/Contents/Author/JustinRichards/Pages/secret_Agent.aspx?objId=40653 to print it out.

Your secret agent name is the name of the first street you lived on, so if you lived on Greenhill Lane you would be Agent Greenhill. Your agent code is your age, plus your house number, plus how many brothers and sisters you have. So if your house number is three, you are eight years old and you have two brothers, your number would
be 13.

TIP! Cover your card in sellotape so it doesn't get wet when you're spying in wet conditions.

AGENT ALFIE

Stick a picture of yourself here

AGENT NAME...

AGENT CODE...

COUNTRY...

ASSIGNMENT...

Hedgehog Slab Illusion

Huh?

Well, Mr Cryption might seem to be talking rubbish, but in fact everything he says is in code. Here are some of the code words that Mr Cryption uses together with what they really mean – provided by the Government Rapid Analysis Decoding and Encryption Section (GRADES). Other words have not yet been deciphered – perhaps you can work them out?

You can also use the list to say things in code, like Mr Cryption. But be warned – if you do, no one will know what you are talking about!

Codeword	Meaning
Alert	Letter
Antelopes	Satellite
Anthology	Collection
Artichoke	Watch out
Bananas	Tummy
Bath	Big tub of water

Codeword	Meaning
Binoculars	Colour
Blue	Difficult
Bridges	Dangerous
Butter	Damaged
Cardigans	Success
Carpet	Unexpected
Casement	Enclosed frame
Cashflow	Expensive
Crisis	Envelope
Dilemma	If
Doom	Clever
Enormous	Worked
Extraction	Code-breaking
Fester	No
Flammable	When
Flippers	Flippers
Frosting	Frosting
Garden	Talking
Geography	Need
Gherkin	Outstanding

Codeword	Meaning
Gold	Stay
Golf	Camouflage
Hamster	Teacher
Hat stand	Saucepan
Heart-shaped	Secret
Hedgehog	Quick
Igloo	Completely
Imposter	Blanket
Identity	In
Illusion	Code
Luggage	Responsibility
Mangle	Achievement
Marbles	Brains
Nightmare	Hoorah!
Office	Not good
Pest	Hiding
Phoenix	Again
Pig	Today
Quibble	Better
Rewind	Recover

Codeword Meaning

Codeword	Meaning
Rock	Circumstances
Safety	Pink
Scribble	Message Ends
Shakespeare	Muddled
Slab	Guide
Sleepwalker	Deception
Slingshot	Hurt
Submarine	After school
Tailor	Lessons
Under	Extremely
Vikings	Fake
Violin	Stringed musical instrument
Visible	Detention
Window	Under
Wobble	Badly
Xylophonics	Good morning
Zebra	Black and white striped animal like a horse
Zero	Netting

WAS THAT ME? OOPS!

The Major's Guide to Effective

SABOTAGE

Years of experience have made the Major one of the top sabotage experts in the world. When he was a fully operational agent, the Major once toppled the diabolic dictator Everard Evildraws single-handed - and it was his left hand. (He bumped into the dictator in the supermarket while looking for a tin of baked beans.)

When he gave the opening lecture at the conference for Best Loyal Agents in Harmony (BLAH), the Major brought the house down. By leaning on the wrong pillar. But it's been rebuilt since then.

Now the Major shares some of his secret tips. Just don't let your mum and dad know that you're been taking advice on how to sabotage everything from your brother's bed to a piece of fresh fruit.

And please be assured that the Major has kindly checked this whole section himself to make sure there are no embarrassing spellig mishtaks.

HOW TO SABOTAGE A BED

Operation Apple Pie: Untuck the bottom sheet from the lower end of the bed, and fold it up to the top. If the bed is made with sheets and blankets, just fold the top of the bottom sheet (with me so far?) over the top of the top sheet. If the bed has a duvet, you'll need to fold it over the top of the duvet and hope no one notices.

Then wait for someone to get into bed - and put their foot in it.

The Major's Special Tip – Don't do this to your own bed.

HOW TO SABOTAGE DINNER

Operation Volcano: Best to do this outdoors! Get some flour and make it into a small mountain on a plate. You only need about a cupful. Make a dent in the top with your finger, and into this add one teaspoon of baking powder. Right, now stand well back and - at arm's length - tip a teaspoon of vinegar on to the top of the baking powder. Then wait for the eruption.

The Major's Special Tip – Don't try this with a bucket of flour, a cup of baking powder and a whole bottle of vinegar. And certainly don't tell Mrs Nuffink that anything like that happened in her classroom that day all the windows got blown out!

HOW TO SABOTAGE A BANANA

Operation Banana Surprise: Peel the banana, being careful that the banana peel all stays attached. Best if you don't have too many strips of peel. Now remove the banana from the inside. You can eat it if you want – lovely with ice cream and very good for you! Now, get some cotton wool or something similar, and roll it into the same size and shape as the original banana. Put it inside the peel, and fold the peel back up. With a needle and thread, very carefully sew the peel back together. Now wait for someone to try to eat the banana...

The Major's Special Tip – Don't get muddled up and eat the cotton wool instead of the real banana. That's not so nice, even with ice cream.

HOW TO SABOTAGE A FIZZY DRINK

Operation Spray: Another one to do outdoors! Unscrew the top of the drinks bottle. Standing well back, drop in a couple

of mints – those oval-shaped ones with a
hard outer shell work best. Now get out
of the way before it goes off!

The Major's Special Tip – Don't hang about or you'll get soaked!

HOW TO SABOTAGE A BOOK

Operation Jumble: If you get this right,
it will jumble up all the letters on the
last few lines of the last page of a
book. It's very spectacular, and actually
very easy. All you need to do is hjks
kiopd uh gjtmxshio jhkda – djskd sjklsa
gstl Mr Cryption Xhjka jkds jfron s

hmds

jkcscvlj

klsd

ocpdioan

clkjdy

skvcjjk

jk

okp

hjk

jkls

Read on for a super-secret sneak preview of Agent Alfie's third adventure: *Licence to Fish!*

On the way to the lake to look for the monster Mr Trick had told them about, Alfie, Harry, Beth and Jack, walked along the edge of the main playing field. A little old lady was standing meekly in the middle of a dozen sixth formers who were lying flat on their backs groaning in pain.

One of the sixth formers struggled to his feet. Only to be knocked down again by a flying jump kick from the little old lady, accompanied by a fierce Ninja attack cry.

"I don't know if they'll be up to Fishing Club," said Jack. "Not after Assassination

Techniques with Miss Fortune."

"If Rod and Annette are there, I'm definitely asking if I can do extra fishing," Harry said.

The sun was low in the sky, glinting on the surface of the lake. It made it difficult to see if there was a monster rising up from the depths. But there was *something* – a huge, dark shape floating on the water.

"Duck!" Jack said.

Alfie, Harry and Beth ducked.

Jack stared at them in surprise. "No," he said, urgently. "Big duck!"

They flung themselves to the ground.

Jack frowned. "There, in the lake." He pointed to the huge dark shape. "There's a big duck in the lake."

From where he was now lying on the wet

grass, Alfie could see that the shape was indeed a big duck. In fact, an enormous duck. It was about two metres tall. And bright yellow.

"You think that's the monster?" Beth asked. "It's not grey. Mr Trick said the monster in the lake was grey."

"It's just a duck," Harry said.

"Big duck," Alfie pointed out.

"Don't you start," Beth said.

"I bet that's what Mr Trick saw," said Jack. "He saw a big duck and thought it was a monster."

Alfie wasn't convinced. "I don't think a long-necked grey monster would look like a big yellow duck."

"No," Harry agreed. "I think it would look more like that." He pointed at the lake.

Alfie and the others had to shield their eyes from the sun to see what he was pointing at.

It was an enormous, grey monster. Its long neck was rising up out of the water, in front of the duck, looming over it – ready to strike. When the monster slowly sank out of sight, the duck was gone.

"Yes," Alfie said. "Exactly like that."

"Where did the duck go?" Beth asked.

"The monster ate it," said Jack. "Better not tell Alice!"

Harry was still shielding his eyes from the sun and looking down towards the edge of the lake. "There's Rod and Annette."

"Maybe they saw the duck and know where it went," Alfie said. "Or the monster."

"I'm going to ask them," Harry decided. He ran off towards the lake shore.

The others waited as Harry spoke briefly to Rod and Annette – still both in their suits and dark glasses.

"You think they really are working for SPUD?" Beth asked.

"Got to be, dressed like that," Jack said confidently.

"Maybe," Alfie said. "They don't look like they usually teach fishing, do they? But if they're working for SPUD, what are they doing?"

"Spying on us," Jack said.

"Yeah, right," Beth told him. "They want to know how good we are at fishing. That'll help them in their plans."

"What *are* their plans?" Alfie wondered. "What does SPUD actually want, do you think?"

"Power," Jack told him. "They're always trying to rig elections and replace world leaders with their own agents."

"Loads of money," Beth added. "They rob banks and steal from wealthy countries."

"World domination," Jack said. "The usual."

Harry came running back, out of breath.

"Did you ask them?" Jack demanded. "What did they say?"

"They said I can do extra fishing on Thursday."

"So, you didn't ask if they saw the monster, then?" Alfie said.

"Or where that poor thing went," Beth added.

"Where what poor thing went?"

"Duck, Harry!" Jack told him. "Big duck!"

"Get up Harry," said Beth. "That's not what he meant."